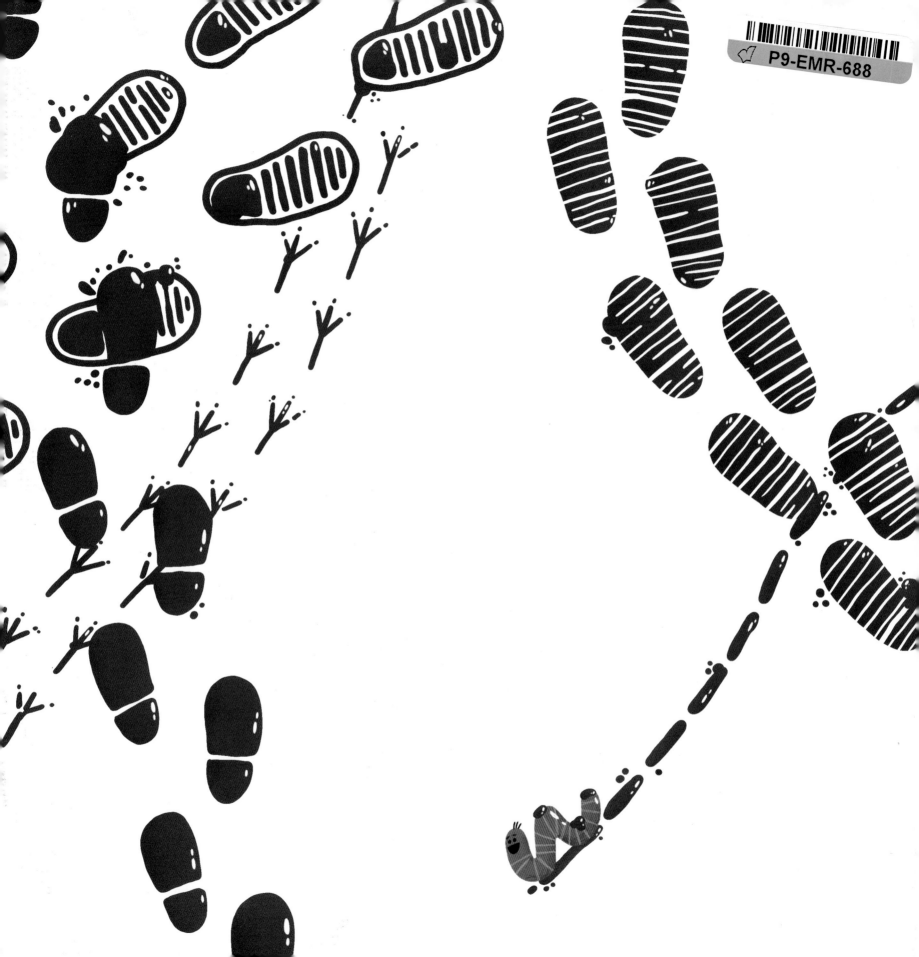

This book is dedicated to all **PURPLE** people.
Whatever shade, we're glad you're here.

All rights reserved. Published in the United States by Random House Children's Books,
a division of Penguin Random House LLC, New York.

Random House and the colophon are registered trademarks of Penguin Random House LLC.

Visit us on the Web! rhcbooks.com

Educators and librarians, for a variety of teaching tools, visit us at RHTeachersLibrarians.com

Library of Congress Cataloging-in-Publication Data is available upon request.
ISBN 978-0-593-12196-2 (trade) — ISBN 978-0-593-12197-9 (lib. bdg.) —
ISBN 978-0-593-12198-6 (ebook)

MANUFACTURED IN CHINA

10 9 8 7 6

First Edition

The World Needs More PURPLE PEOPLE

By **KRISTEN BELL & BENJAMIN HART**

Hey, kid! I've got a secret! It's gonna knock your socks off! And I can't wait to share it with you....

Illustrations by
DANIEL WISEMAN

Random House 🏠 New York

Ta-da! Follow my guide to become a **PURPLE** person.

Now, you may be asking yourself,
"Why in the whole wide world would
I want to be PURPLE?"

PURPLE is a magic color made when red and blue work together. I think all the best things in the world are PURPLE.

But you're probably wondering, "What does that have to do with PEOPLE?" Wow! Are you a genius? Because you're already on your way to becoming a **PURPLE** person. You want to know why?

STEP 1:
ASK (really great) QUESTIONS

My dad says PURPLE people ask great questions. Questions about EVERYTHING! Even questions about QUESTIONS!

PURPLE questions are the kind that help you learn something really BIG about the world or something really small about another person.

How tall is the world's tallest rainbow?

What's your bear's name?

Charlie.

Dad says the more PURPLE questions you ask, the more PURPLE you become.

How many do you think there are?

He also says I can only ask him twenty questions about space dolphins per day.

My grandma says PURPLE people laugh a lot!

We are always laughing together.

I mean like snot-out-our-nose laughing.

We laugh at books.

We laugh at jokes.

We laugh at donkey dances
and hairy elephant knees.

HEE-HAW!

HAHA-
SNORT-
HAHA

And we ESPECIALLY laugh at Grandpa's funny noises.

PURPLE laughing helps us remember the things we share and forget what we thought made us different. And it's almost impossible to be angry when you are laughing. Try it! I dare you!

Grandma says the more **PURPLE** laughing you do, the more **PURPLE** you become.

She also says Grandpa's noises are her favorite funny noises in the whole wide world.

My mom says **PURPLE** people use their voice and don't lose their voice.

She encourages me to use my voice to sing . . .

to give good ideas . . .

. . . and to share my opinions.

Sometimes people lose their voice. And that's okay. It happens! A **PURPLE** voice helps someone who is having trouble finding their own voice. **PURPLE** people don't just speak up. They also listen!

Maybe you could tell them you don't like it when they call you that name?

Want me to help you tell them?

Mom says the more you use a **PURPLE** voice, the more **PURPLE** you become.

Mom, can you help me with my play?

BY PENNYTON

She also says she heard my opinion on brussels sprouts, but I still have to eat them. I'm gonna work on a better argument.

STEP 4:
WORK HARD
(super-duper hard)

My grandpa says PURPLE people know how to "dig in and get stuff done."

He and I like to work hard while we build things . . .

and while we learn things . . .

BIRDS OF THE NORTHEAST

. . . and while we grow things.

PURPLE work is the kind of work that's done together
to change something that needs changing . . .

What do we want?

MORE PLAYGROUNDS!

When do we want them?

NOW!

fix something that needs fixing . . .

. . . or help someone who needs helping.

Grandpa says the more PURPLE work you do,
the more PURPLE you become.

He also says no purple work has ever been done while sitting on your backside sipping strawberry lemonade.

JUST KIDDING!

That's not the way to become a PURPLE person. Actually, being a PURPLE person has nothing to do with what you look like.

MRS. VIOLET

My teacher says **PURPLE** people look all sorts of ways.

They are big and small, old and young. Some wear cool coats, some wear shorts with lots of pockets, and some wear funny hats. She says some **PURPLE** people feel blue sometimes and red other times. And some **PURPLE** people even have green hair!

So those are my surefire steps to turning into a **PURPLE** pers—

Hey, wait a minute. . . .

★ Y**OU** ask really great questions.

★ Y**OU** laugh a lot.

★ Y**OU** use your voice all the time.

★ Y**OU** are a really hard worker.

★ And Y**OU** are totally YOU!

Well, I'll be a llama's mama!

You've been beautifully PURPLE this WHOLE time!
I sure am glad you're a PURPLE person.

Mama?!

Because the world needs more PURPLE people. Just. Like. You.